The Ghost of
GRACIE MANSION

Susan Kohl

Illustrated by Ned Butterfield

SILVER MOON PRESS
NEW YORK

First Silver Moon Press Edition 1999

The publisher would like to thank David L. Reese, Curator of
Gracie Mansion, and Grady Turner of the New-York Historical Society
for their help in preparing this manuscript.

For information:
Silver Moon Press
New York, NY
(800) 874-3320

Library of Congress Cataloging-in-Publication Data
Kohl, Susan.
The Ghost of Gracie Mansion / Susan Kohl;
illustrated by Ned Butterfield – 1st Silver Moon Press ed.
p. cm. – (Mysteries in Time)
Summary: During a yellow fever epidemic in 1803,
Esther and Archibald Gracie move their family from Manhattan to
their country home, where the children search
for an underground passageway and a mysterious visitor
to the mansion that would later be home
to the mayors of New York City.
ISBN 1-893110-04-4
1. Gracie Mansion (New York, N.Y.) Juvenile fiction. [1. Gracie
Mansion (New York, N.Y.) Fiction. 2. New York (State)–History–1775-1865
Fiction. 3. Mystery and detective stories.]
I. Butterfield, Ned, ill. II. Title. III. Series.
PZ7.K82444 Gh 1999
[Fic] - - dc21
99-13049
CIP

10 9 8 7 6 5 4 3 2 1

Printed in the USA

1

DISTRACTED BY THOUGHTS OF A TRIP HE DIDN'T want to take, sixteen-year-old William stood up too fast, bumping his head on the slanted ceiling of his room. "Ouch!" he cried, mussing his thick, dark hair as he rubbed his head. He looked around the room he shared with his younger brother Archie. The floor was littered with large trunks he was supposed to be filling with his belongings, and clothing and blankets were stacked on the beds. He tossed a shirt into one of the cloth bags and scowled when he missed. Still rubbing his head, he walked over to the window and looked wistfully at the busy street below.

"Jasper!" he called out, recognizing a messenger he knew. He banged on the window, but it was useless. Broadway was much too noisy with clomping horse hoofs, squeaking wheels, and noisy bells.

"Hot pastries! Hot buns!" called a crusty old vendor below his window, standing next to a large puddle from yesterday's rain.

William slid open the window and felt the unseasonably warm May air. "Jasper!" he called again, but his friend had already disappeared down the street.

William wished he was out in the hustle and bustle of the morning. The spring of 1803 was a very exciting time to be in New York City, which was well on its way to becoming the business center and main port of the United States. For the past two years, William had worked as a messenger for his father, Archibald Gracie, a leading commission merchant and ship owner. Mr. Gracie owned twenty-one ships, including schooners, brigs, and other vessels. The ships brought goods from England and France to New York, and then restocked them with goods from the Caribbean Islands to take back to Europe. From the time he was five, William had looked forward to working with his father. Though being a messenger was only a starting job, he took it very seriously, delivering notes and letters from his father to bankers, lawyers, and other merchants. He hoped one day he'd be as important as his father.

In addition to being a merchant and ship owner, Mr. Gracie was on the directing boards of several banks and insurance companies, and vice president of the Chamber of Commerce. Like many other businessmen, he worked from the Gracie's home on Broadway, the main thoroughfare running north and south. The house was very close to the most important part of the city—Pearl, Water, and Front Streets, and the wharves and slips along the East River.

I bet Jasper's on his way to the Tontine Coffee House where all the action is, William thought, enviously. The Tontine Coffee House on Water Street was always crowded with merchants and brokers making deals with each other, the constant din of voices in the air. Though William often didn't understand

2

what was being said, he knew that if he stayed long enough things would start to make sense. *Now that we're leaving the city I'll never learn*, he thought miserably. He feared that moving out of New York would ruin all his plans for the future.

For months, he'd been looking forward to this spring when his father had planned to promote him to clerk. Clerks copied lists of merchandise that would be available once each ship arrived and unloaded its goods, and organized arrival and departure timetables for the ships while in New York Harbor. But now that the yellow fever epidemic had broken out in New York City, the Gracies were moving to their new country home at Horn's Hook to escape the disease.

William had to admit he was excited about seeing how the house looked now that more construction had been done. It had taken several years to build and he hadn't seen it since the previous summer when the Gracies had gone for a two-week holiday. But as much as he wanted to see it, he certainly didn't want to live that far from the city.

Thump! Thump! Thump! The familiar sound of drums brought William away from his thoughts. His heart sank as he watched a big black carriage pulled by four horses moving down the street. Another funeral was in progress!

"Drat it all!" he said aloud, running a hand through his dark brown hair. Another reminder of the yellow fever epidemic. It seemed like every day they heard about another house that was invaded

3

by the epidemic. No one knew what had caused the disease though some suspected the Collect had something to do with it. The Collect was a large pond in lower Manhattan that was now said to *collect* only foul smells and mosquitoes.

William turned away from the noisy scene outside to the eerily quiet house. Usually the upstairs rooms were filled with the noise of a large family while the downstairs rooms were busy with his father's business associates. William wondered how his father planned to work from Horn's Hook. After all, it was very far from New York Harbor, the center of the action. He had wanted to ask him about it but, lately, his father had been busier than ever.

"Are you finished packing yet, William?" Mrs. Gracie called from downstairs.

"Almost," called William, carelessly tossing a pair of trousers onto a half-filled cloth bag.

"It doesn't look like it," said eight-year-old Archie who had quietly slipped into the room. Archibald Gracie, Jr. had been named after his father, but everyone called him Archie.

"Sometimes you can be a real pest, Archie," William grumbled. Noticing Archie's hurt expression, William softened his tone and ruffled his brother's soft, brown hair. "How about helping me fill these trunks?"

Happy with the chance to help his older brother, Archie speedily began filling them with clothing. William worked in silence.

"William, why don't you want to go to Horn's

Hook?" asked Archie, pushing a filled trunk toward the door. "Mama says we can ride horses, go for boat rides, and climb trees. Won't that be fun?"

"It'll be fun for you, Archie," William said, not wanting to hurt his brother's feelings, "but I'm a bit old for those things. Horn's Hook is a nice place to go on holiday but not to live. I'd much rather be living and working in downtown Manhattan."

"Oh," Archie said, shrugging.

Suddenly, twelve-year-old Sarah burst into the room carrying a china doll. Her pale face was wet with tears.

"What's wrong, Sarah?" William asked. "Why aren't you downstairs helping Mama and Eliza with the packing?"

"Because she doesn't know *how* to pack up our own room," said fourteen-year-old Eliza, who now stood in the doorway. Though she and Sarah resembled each other, Eliza had a thinner face, a pointier nose, and curlier brown hair. "Mama said we should only bring the things we need, but Sarah wants to take everything—including that silly china doll. It's just a useless decoration."

"Eliza, can't you be a little more understanding?" William said. He was used to settling arguments between his sisters. "I remember when you used to carry a rag doll everywhere you went."

"When I was eight, not twelve!" said Eliza, tossing her curls behind her shoulder. "Sarah's too old for dolls."

"Not china dolls!" said Sarah. "Rebecca Anne

watches over me when I sleep."

"In your imagination!" said Eliza.

"What's wrong with my imagination?" wondered Sarah.

"Nothing," said William. Ever since he could remember, Sarah had been making up stories. When she wasn't telling stories, she was reading.

"What does Mama think?" asked William.

"About what?" called Esther Gracie from the bottom of the stairway. Mrs. Gracie was labeling trunks in the front hall.

"Nothing," Sarah and Eliza said together, not wanting to bother their mother.

"Mama, is there anything I can do for you?" called William. "The girls don't seem to be much help."

"William, stop acting like you're the only helper in the house," Eliza hissed. "I spent all day yesterday helping Mama and Lizzie pack up the kitchen. That's more than you've done. All you've been doing is worrying Mama by sulking about wanting to stay in the city."

"The only reason you're excited to go is because cousin James is going to be there," said William.

"That's not true!" Eliza said, blushing.

But William knew it was. The last time they had been with their cousins he had noticed a difference in Eliza when she was around their cousin James, a handsome boy two years older than she. His mother, Elizabeth Lambert, and Esther Gracie were sisters. They also had several brothers with large families as well. Sometimes the Gracie children spent so much time with their cousins it seemed as if they were all one family. The Lamberts would be staying at a house only a few minutes away from Horn's Hook.

"Children, stop arguing!" called Mrs. Gracie. "If you're finished packing up your rooms, I could use your help down here."

William followed Eliza and Sarah downstairs, leaving Archie to finish packing his belongings. They found their mother in the front hall, surrounded by trunks, with fresh tears sliding down her angular cheeks. Her wavy brown hair was tied up in a bun with loose strands hanging down.

"We're sorry we upset you, Mama," said Sarah.

"It's not you," said Mrs. Gracie. She held up two miniature portraits for the children to see. "I still miss these sweet babies who died so young. I'm so thankful that you are all healthy and I want to keep it that way. Diseases like yellow fever are impossible to control. That's why I want to get you away from this crowded city as soon as possible."

While Eliza and Sarah wrapped the miniatures in soft cloth and placed them carefully in a trunk filled with linens, Mrs. Gracie wiped her eyes with a handkerchief. "I hope I've made the right decision to leave. It's not the ideal situation for your father's business."

"I thought Papa agreed it was sensible to leave," said Eliza.

"He does," said Mrs. Gracie. "But it means he has to reorganize his business so he can work from

Horn's Hook." Suddenly they heard clomping and clattering outside on the cobblestones. "Speaking of your father, I hear the carriage and wagon out front. William, why don't you go help your father load the wagon while Sarah and Eliza finish with these trunks."

William opened the front door and was confronted by a waft of warm air. His father stood outside the closed carriage talking to the driver. Behind the carriage was a large, open wagon. Three stray dogs and a pig were sniffing at a puddle on the opposite side of the street.

"Hi, Papa!" Archie called from their second-floor bedroom window. Mr. Gracie looked up and waved. "I'm coming down to help."

Before walking over to the wagon, William looked down Broadway toward Trinity Church. Its windows shimmered in the sunshine. The church had been completely destroyed during the Revolutionary War and then rebuilt in 1790, three years before the Gracies moved from Virginia to New York. The reconstruction of the church had been a sign that the city, which had been very important before the war, was going to be just as important after the war. *There are no churches near Horn's Hook*, William thought. *It was far away from everything.*

"Ready to load the wagon?" Mr. Gracie asked, leaving the carriage driver to water the two horses.

"I'm ready," said William, following his father into the house. Mr. Gracie was a tall, elegant gentleman. Although he was modern in his ways of thinking, he

still wore the traditional merchants' clothing of the previous generation: white stockings and dark brown breeches. His hair was loosely tied back with a black ribbon. He carried a three-cornered hat under his arm. Though William dressed in a more modern style, with short hair and tightly-fitted trousers tucked into his boots the way young men of his age wore them, he hoped he'd grow up to be exactly like his father.

"How can I help?" Archie asked, breathless from running down the stairs.

William pointed out the trunks and parcels that were ready to be loaded onto the wagon and the three of them got to work. Mr. Gracie and William carried the heavier loads, Archie the light ones. William had hoped to ask his father how he planned to work at Horn's Hook, but they were so busy he decided it would have to wait.

BY NOON, THE WAGON WAS loaded and the Gracies were ready to leave. Mrs. Gracie and Lizzie, the housekeeper, each carrying one of the toddlers, climbed into the carriage first. William noticed how different Lizzie looked from the Gracies with her red hair and freckles. While Eliza was climbing into the carriage behind them, William remembered that he'd left his favorite quill up in his room.

"I'll be right back," he said, heading toward the house.

"Tell Sarah to hurry up," said Mrs. Gracie. "I want to get away from the unhealthy city air as soon as possible. Two of the Parker children just took ill, and the youngest Martin child died this morning." Everyone was silent.

William found Sarah in the room she shared with Eliza, saying good-bye to the pictures on the walls, the water pitcher with the crack in it, and the stone frog on the dresser. Aside from that, the room was almost empty.

"Come on, Sarah," said William. "We're ready to go."

"I'm really not a baby," Sarah said, turning to him. "I just grow very attached to things."

"I do too, Sarah," William said gently. "I'm attached to New York City. But Mama and Papa think it best that we go." He found his quill and the two of them went downstairs. As soon as they squeezed into the crowded carriage, the driver flicked the reins, the horses whinnied, and they headed north on Broadway. *Away from all the action*, William thought sadly.

2

THE FIVE-MILE TRIP TO HORN'S HOOK WOULDN'T have taken more than two hours if the road had been paved. But Broadway's cobblestone paving ended at Tenth Street. From there on, the Gracies traveled over muddy roads with deep holes.

"Hold on!" Archie cried as they went over a bump.

William and the others held tightly to the leather straps inside as the carriage bounced along.

"I feel sorry for the horses," said Eliza.

I feel sorry for my life, thought William, cramped between Lizzie, who had two-year-old Robert on her lap, and Sarah. Archie sat on the other side of Sarah. Across from them were Mr. and Mrs. Gracie and Eliza, who held one-year-old Esther, known to everyone as Hettie, on her lap. As they headed north, Archie, Sarah, and Eliza gazed out the window, announcing everything they passed. William wished he were next to a window, but he knew better than to complain.

"I'm hungry," said Archie, after they'd been riding only a half hour.

"So am I," said Sarah, "and I wish Archie would stop kicking me."

"I'm not doing it on purpose," said Archie. "Blame it on the bumps."

"How about some ginger biscuits?" said Lizzie, reaching down for the tin container she'd brought.

"Yes!" shouted Sarah and Archie. Though Mr. Gracie had hired Lizzie for her skills at caring for young children, she'd turned out to be a wonderful cook. They had discovered this two weeks earlier when their own cook went home to Boston to take care of a sick brother. Mrs. Gracie had been very upset by the loss of their cook—especially with all the work to do before they left—and she hadn't had a chance to look for a new one. That's when Lizzie came to the rescue and prepared a meal tastier than any meal the cook had ever made! From then on, Mrs. Gracie, Eliza, and Sarah helped out with the younger children so Lizzie could prepare their meals. Eventually they'd have to hire someone else, but for now they managed.

Just as Lizzie removed the tin lid, the carriage went over a bump and several biscuits fell out of the container.

"Flying biscuits!" said Sarah, laughing. "They're magic!"

"That's an interesting way of looking at it, Sarah," said Mr. Gracie. "But I wonder if anything can be done about having these roads paved. People are using them more and more these days."

"I heard two men in the Tontine Coffee House talking about the new street commissioners and the poor condition of the roads," said William.

"Yes," said Mr. Gracie, "the first street commissioners were appointed five years ago. I hope something can be done because some day New York City will be much bigger than we know it to be now."

"Papa, are you going to work at Horn's Hook as much as you do in the city?" Archie asked, munching on a biscuit.

"Close your mouth when you chew!" Eliza said, making a face.

When did Eliza start to act like a bossy grown-up? William wondered, looking at his sister. He had to admit she was turning into a pretty young lady, with delicate features and shiny brown curls. Though Sarah was only two years younger than Eliza, she still looked like a child with shoulder-length brown hair that was always messy. But he was much too interested in his father's answer to give his sisters any more thought.

"Yes, Archie, I'll be working from sun up," said Mr. Gracie. "But I'll make time for some fun as well."

"How will you work so far away from New York Harbor?" William asked, relieved finally to have the chance to talk about business with his father.

"The same way I work in the city," said Mr. Gracie. "The captains of our ships will have been given instructions to stop at Horn's Hook after they reach New York Harbor. Our property faces the narrowest part of the East River. In spite of the dangerous currents, our captains ought to be able to drop anchor there. You can help me prepare timetables and cargo lists."

"Like a clerk?" asked William, hoping he had heard correctly.

"You didn't think I was planning on doing it alone, did you?" Mr. Gracie said, wiping his brow with a handkerchief. "I expect Alexander Hamilton will be up to see us in a week or two with some important legal information."

William felt especially proud of his father's friendship with Alexander Hamilton, a very important New York lawyer. Mr. Hamilton had also played an important role in the United States government. Whenever he came to the Gracie house to discuss business or to play cards with his father, he treated William like a grown-up. Last time they'd seen each other, Mr. Hamilton had told him about the country home he was having built in Harlem, which was even farther north than Horn's Hook.

"I'm thirsty," whined Archie.

"I brought a crock of lemonade, but I'm afraid it will spill with all these bumps," said Lizzie, shifting Robert to her other leg. Despite the noise and bumps he was sleeping soundly. Hettie, on the other hand, now on Mrs. Gracie's lap, was whimpering.

"We'll make a fresh pitcher of lemonade as soon as we get there," said Mrs. Gracie, as they turned onto Old Post Road."

"This used to be an Indian trail," said William.

"Really?" said Sarah. "Maybe the Indians are still here spying on us."

"Here comes another story," said Eliza, rolling her eyes.

"Let's have Papa tell us a story," said William, hoping to distract Sarah and Eliza from getting into an argument. "A real story about the history of Horn's Hook."

"Good idea," said Mrs. Gracie, looking at her husband.

"Well, I don't know everything that happened at Horn's Hook," Mr. Gracie began, "but I'll tell you what I do know. I know there was fighting on our property during the war.

"The War of Independence or the Revolutionary War?" asked Archie, trying to remember what he'd learned in school.

"They were both the same war," said William. "It was called the War of Independence by the people who wanted to be free from England and its king, and it was called the Revolutionary War by the English and people who were loyal to England. They were called Loyalists."

"Why did they decide to fight on our property?" asked Sarah.

"Our property begins just after the most turbulent part of the river," Mr. Gracie explained. "Because it's the narrowest part of the river, it's easy to fortify. That's why the land around Horn's Hook has always been strategically important to New York. A fort was built there to protect the river route. Once the war began, this fort became even more important."

"Who was in control of Horn's Hook? The Loyalists or the Americans?" asked Archie.

"Sometimes it was in the hands of the Loyalists. At other times it was in the hands of the Americans, or Rebels, as they were called," William explained, realizing how much more he knew than his brother and sisters.

"Anyway," said Mr. Gracie, "there was a house on the property belonging to the Waltons, a Loyalist family. I bought the property from the Waltons when I first came to New York, but by that time their house had been torn down and they were living across the river. They had moved there to get away from all the fighting. In fact, we used the foundation of the Walton house for our own basement."

"Did they tear the house down while the Waltons were living there?" asked Archie.

"No," said Mr. Gracie. "The Waltons had to leave when the house was taken over by the Rebels."

"And once they left," said Mrs. Gracie, "the beautiful house they'd built was bombarded by English soldiers and completely destroyed."

"That doesn't seem fair," said Sarah. "If the Waltons were loyal to the English King, why was their house destroyed by English soldiers?"

"Because the English soldiers were trying to get it back from the Rebels, without caring who lived in the house," said Mr. Gracie, "which points out how war can hurt people no matter what they believe."

"Who told you all of this?" asked Archie.

"An English lieutenant named Robertson," said Mr. Gracie. "His job was to order the bombardment of the fort that the Rebels had built. He was a very careful man and, before any shooting began, he drew pictures of the house and described it on paper. He wrote that it had double chimneys and sloping lawns."

"When we get to the house, I'll show you one of Robertson's watercolors that's hanging in the parlor," said Mrs. Gracie. "It's a view from Horn's Hook."

Just then they went over the biggest bump yet and Archie fell out of his seat.

Oh no, thought William. *He's going to start crying.*

But Archie surprised everyone by laughing as Sarah helped him climb back onto the seat. "So what else happened?" he asked.

Mr. Gracie continued. "Eventually, the English got the property back and kept it until after the war was over. Then they turned it over to the Rebels on Evacuation Day in 1783. That was the day the King of England officially removed his troops from New York."

"Were the English still here when you arrived?" William asked his father.

"I actually got here five months after Evacuation Day, but I didn't stay in New York," said Mr. Gracie. "It was very hard to do business here then. It was easier to establish my operation in Virginia."

"But if he hadn't stayed in New York for those few months, then he wouldn't have met me," said Mrs. Gracie, smiling fondly at her husband.

"That's true," said Mr. Gracie, smiling at his wife. "And none of you would have been born."

"Weren't the Waltons sad to leave the house?" asked Eliza.

"We were told that Mrs. Walton cried when she heard that the Americans were in control and she and her family would have to go." said Mrs. Gracie. "She had loved the place so much she called it 'her fair heart's desire.' Soon after they left, Mrs. Walton became ill and never recovered. She died on August 1, 1782, and Mr. Walton died eight days later."

"What a sad story," said Sarah. "Maybe Mrs. Walton's ghost is still living in the house."

"Oh Sarah," said Eliza. "You're so silly. There's no such thing as ghosts."

"There may not be any ghosts," said Mr. Gracie, "but there *is* a secret underground passageway in the basement."

"Really!" said William, unable to hide his surprise. The others were just as intrigued. "You never told me about a secret passageway, Papa."

"Where is it?" asked Eliza.

"I'm not sure of the exact spot," said Mr. Gracie, "but supposedly it leads from the old foundation to the river. The Waltons had it built in case they had to make a quick escape. I don't know if they ever had to use it."

"Have you ever found it?" asked William.

Mr. Gracie shook his head. "I asked the carpenter to look for it when we started construction, but if he found it he never told me. It would be somewhere in the basement, right near the kitchen or possibly near the wine cellar. There's a good chance it's still there, but I'm not sure where."

"I can't wait to explore!" said Sarah.

"Me too," said Eliza.

"Let's search every inch of the basement," said Archie. "Will you help too, William?"

"Maybe I'll help out when I'm not working," William said, trying to hide his excitement. But he had to admit, he was just as curious as his brother and sisters.

"There's a lot of work to be done first," said Mrs. Gracie. "It'll take us a few days to get settled."

"I see the river!" cried Archie, looking out the window.

William and the others craned their necks to see through the windows on the east side of the carriage. The river looked like a bright blue ribbon, threaded through the trees. Although they were a good distance from the water, they could see many ships passing by.

"We're almost there!" said Sarah.

Everyone was silent as the carriage turned onto the private road leading to Horn's Hook. As glimpses of the house came into view between the trees, they all gasped in amazement. Even William hadn't expected what stood before them.

"THIS ISN'T A HOUSE," SAID ELIZA, AS THE house came into view. "It's a mansion!"

William had to agree with his sister as the carriage followed the private drive to the front of the property. The yellow, two-story frame house with green shutters, the lawn and gardens surrounding it, and the view of the river beyond was truly a beautiful sight. White railings surrounded the large open porch, filled with chairs and a table, and the sloping roof from which four tall white chimneys rose. The rich, green lawn, with flower gardens along its edges, sloped gently down to another set of railings. Surrounding everything were tall, lush trees with leaves of different shades of green.

"It looks completely different from when we were here last year," William said with awe.

"It looks as if it were built for a king and a queen," said Sarah. "Let's call it Gracies' Mansion."

"I like the sound of that," said Archie.

"Me too," said William, surprised at his change in mood. The scent of pine and the gentle breeze made him forget New York City for a few moments. He had to admit he welcomed the sound of chirping birds for a change. It sure beat the drumming of a funeral procession.

"Will I have my own bedroom?" Eliza asked, looking toward the windows.

"You all will," said Mr. Gracie. "And there are two guest rooms as well so you won't have to give up your rooms when we have overnight visitors."

"But I *like* sharing a room with William," said Archie.

"That's because you don't know what it's like to have your own room," William said, trying to sound convincing. "Try it for a couple nights. If you don't like it, you can stay in my room."

"Okay," said Archie. "I guess I'm getting to be a big boy." Smiling, Mr. Gracie leaned forward and patted Archie on the knee.

"I can't wait to see my bedroom," said Sarah. "I'll bet it looks like a princess's room."

The carriage finally came to a halt. As soon as the driver opened the door, Archie, Sarah, and Eliza climbed out. William followed.

"I'll race you to the river, William," Archie said, his legs already in position.

"Not now," said William. "I have to unload the wagon."

"*I'll* race you," Sarah said to Archie, sprinting ahead of him."

"That's not fair!" said Archie, trying to catch up.

"Don't go past the railing," Mrs. Gracie called, trying not to disturb Hettie, who was now sleeping peacefully in her arms. "And hurry back. We've got much to do."

"If you don't want us going close to the river," said Eliza, watching her brother and sisters race, "how are we going to bathe?"

"It's safe to bathe by the cove," said Mr. Gracie, still in the carriage helping Lizzie down. "Remember where you swam last summer? The cove is at the northernmost part of the property and has a little beach."

"It's so tranquil here," said Lizzie, reaching out for Robert to be handed down to her by Mr. Gracie. "Doesn't Horn's Hook remind you of Dumfries, Mr. Gracie?"

"That's exactly what I thought when I first saw the property," said Mr. Gracie. Dumfries, Scotland, was the original home town of Mr. Gracie.

Like his brother and sisters, William felt a strong urge to explore. *But exploring is for children*, he thought. *And I'm not a child anymore.*

"I won!" Sarah called from the top of the hill leading down to the riverbank.

"You had a head start!" cried Archie.

"Eliza," said Mrs. Gracie. "Please get your brother and sister back here. Tell them they can play later."

As Eliza headed toward the river, a sturdily-built man, with a slight limp and silky white hair pulled back like Mr. Gracie's, came out of the house to greet the family. Mr. Gracie introduced him as Henry Fellows, the caretaker of the property. He and his wife lived in a small cabin less than a quarter of a mile away.

"Welcome," he said. "I hope you're all hungry. I

bought a week's supply of provisions yesterday as you requested. My wife has prepared tea, lemonade, and sandwiches for you to have out on the porch. She's already set the table."

"Isn't she a dear!" said Mrs. Gracie. "Before I do anything I must go inside and thank her."

"She left a few minutes ago to prepare tea for our own family," said Henry. "But I'll send your good wishes."

"Very well," said Mrs. Gracie. "William, Archibald, you can unload the wagon later. The driver won't be leaving for another hour. He has to water the horses and have something to eat himself. Let's go eat what Mrs. Fellows has prepared for us."

William and Mr. Gracie followed Mrs. Gracie, Lizzie and the young ones, up the porch steps and through the front doors. Eliza, Sarah, and Archie burst through the door after them.

"I love it here!" said Sarah. "It's perfect."

Willliam felt just as excited as Sarah though he didn't show it. *After all, I still want to go back to the city*, he told himself.

The front hall of the house was just as exquisite as the outside with shiny pine and chestnut floors, a majestic curved stairway with a polished banister, and tasteful pictures adorning the walls. To the right was a spacious dining room with a long table and a light blue rug. To the left was a large front parlor, which opened into the front hall, and was crowded with well-made chairs and tables that looked inviting and comfortable. The drawn drapes kept the room

cool and dim, and the patterned rug added a subtle splash of color. Precious knickknacks, mostly related to ships and the sea, were spread out on the wooden mantle above the large fireplace.

"I had no idea it would be this nice," William said with surprise.

"I hoped you'd like it, William," said Mr. Gracie. "I

know you didn't want to come."

William felt his face flush. He knew he hadn't been in very good spirits lately but didn't realize his father had noticed. He didn't want him to think he was ungrateful for having such a grand country house to live in.

"It's not that," said William. "I just . . . "

"I want to show you something," said Mr. Gracie, leading William away from the others. William followed his father down a narrow hallway and into a small parlor toward the north end of the house.

"What a great view!" said William, going straight to one of the three large windows facing the East River. Since the house was above the river, they could see for miles, northward and southward. "I didn't realize how many ships would be passing by."

"I told you, William," Mr. Gracie said, smiling, "all sailing vessels coming from Europe can easily pass by here after entering New York Harbor. That's why I chose this room for our study.

"*Our* study?" William asked, turning to face his father who was gesturing toward a desk. For the first time, he noticed two identical desks, each facing a window. Each desk had a chair beside it for visitors.

"Which desk would you like?" asked Mr. Gracie.

William was speechless. He certainly hadn't expected to have his own desk. If he had stayed in New York City, he wouldn't have had a desk for a few more years.

"How about this one?" Mr. Gracie said with a twinkle in his eye, pointing to the desk on the right.

"Sure," said William, still overwhelmed. He sat in his new desk chair and opened the top drawer. A brand new quill lay inside.

"Archibald! William! Come have some tea!" Mrs. Gracie called from the kitchen downstairs in the cellar.

"We're coming, Esther!" called Mr. Gracie. Then he turned to William. "We'll start working bright and early tomorrow morning," said Mr. Gracie. "How does that sound?"

"Great," said William. As he followed his father out into the hall, he took one last look out the windows. *Jasper and the other messengers would never believe this*, he thought proudly.

William hadn't realized how hungry he was until he saw the plate of sandwiches on the porch table. He chose a sandwich, sat down in a white windsor chair next to Eliza, and began to eat.

"What a great view," said Eliza. "I like the way our property curves into a calm, protected cove."

"It's not very calm over there," Sarah said, pointing north toward the spot where the Harlem River flowed into the East River. The water was churning violently as a large brig tried to get through.

"That rough, turbulent part of the river is called Hell Gate," said Mr. Gracie.

"That sounds scary," said Sarah. "Why don't they call it something pretty like "Bell Gate" or "Well Gate"?"

"Because they don't have your imagination, Sarah," said Eliza, laughing.

"I know why," said William, remembering something he had learned in school. "It's called Hell Gate because there were lots of shipwrecks there."

"Then there's no way I'm going to go boating while we're here," said Eliza, pushing a curl away from her face.

"Me neither," Sarah agreed. "I'd rather ride horses. In fact, I want to go down to the stables this afternoon." The stables, which housed three horses and a pony, were at the southeast edge of the property.

"Can any of you tell me why Horn's Hook was so important during the war?" Mr. Gracie asked, looking at his three older children.

"Because it's easy to see what's happening on the ships passing by and across the river on the Long Island shore," said William. "I bet that I can throw a rock from our side of the river to the other."

"It might be a little too far for that," said Mr. Gracie, "but you're right about our great viewpoint."

"I can see sailors on that ship," Eliza said, pointing toward a schooner with two masts. "Is that the cove where we'll be swimming, Papa?"

"That's it," said Mr. Gracie. "We'll have to wait a week or so. The water is still a bit cold."

"I can see people on the opposite shore," said Sarah. "I wonder if they can see *us*."

"They probably can't," said Mr. Gracie. "That's General Stevens' house. Our property is surrounded by big, old trees—another reason this is such a strategic location—so they probably can't see us here on the porch."

William gladly accepted a mug of freshly brewed

tea from Mrs. Gracie, who sat down across from him.

"Are we expecting a lot of guests, Papa?" asked Sarah.

"Papa will be having lots of visitors," said William, "including Mr. Hamilton."

"We can also invite our cousins over for tea," Eliza suggested, giving William a warning look. He decided against teasing her.

"I have a feeling we're going to have a lot of nice afternoons on this porch," said Mrs. Gracie.

"I've really looked forward to this," said Mr. Gracie, putting his plate on a side table. "Being in the country . . . sitting on the porch with my family . . . relaxing for a change. I feel terrible that I've missed so many meals lately."

"Speaking of missing meals," said William, "where's Archie? He never misses a meal."

"I don't know," said Mrs. Gracie. "Archie!" she called. There was no answer. "I'm going to see if he's inside with Lizzie and the little ones," she said, standing up.

"Eliza, why don't we see if your brother went over to the river," said Mr. Gracie. "I think we're going to have to make some rules around here. This part of the river can be dangerous."

As soon as they left, William stood up. "I'm going to start unloading the wagon," he said to Sarah.

"I'll bring these plates down into the kitchen," Sarah said. "I'm sure Lizzie has her hands full.

On his way to the wagon, William thought he heard someone whispering his name. He stopped walking and listened closely. It was coming from above. He looked up into the branches of an oak tree and saw some rustling leaves, then a foot dangling from a branch.

"It's me, William!" Archie called in a low voice.

"Archie!" William said, sternly. "Come down from there. Everyone's worried about you."

"I can't!" said Archie. "I climbed too high and didn't want Mama and Papa to get mad. I waited for you to come unload the wagon."

As William climbed toward Archie, he remembered what fun he'd had climbing trees as a child. Maybe, if he had the time, he decided, he'd climb just one tree. Standing on a low branch, he reached up, and grabbed Archie.

"Thanks, William," said Archie. "Please don't tell anyone that I got stuck up here. Then Mama will never let me climb a tree again."

"They're going to wonder where you were," said William. "What do you want me to say?"

Before Archie could answer, they heard a shriek from the house. It was Sarah. Forgetting the tree, forgetting the wagon, William and Archie raced toward the house.

4

JUST AS WILLIAM AND ARCHIE REACHED THE house, Sarah burst through the doorway onto the porch. She looked pale and shaky.

"What's wrong, Sarah?" asked Mrs. Gracie, following her daughter through the porch door. When she saw Sarah shaking, she hugged her close. "You poor thing. What happened?"

"S- s- someone was in the house," said Sarah, her eyes wide with fear. "I . . . I . . . "

"There's my boy!" they heard Mr. Gracie say as he and Eliza walked toward Archie from the riverbank.

"Where were you, Archie?" asked Eliza, breathless from the steep climb. But when she saw Sarah's face, she didn't wait for an answer.

"What's wrong, Sarah?" asked Eliza.

"I was going back and forth from the porch into the house, bringing in the plates and mugs and the rest of the sandwiches," said Sarah, trying to remember every detail. "The second time . . . no maybe the third time . . . I came inside and saw someone rushing down the stairs toward the kitchen."

"Are you sure you're not imagining things?" asked Eliza.

William had been thinking the same thing, but he

knew how sensitive Sarah became when people didn't believe her.

"No," said Sarah, shaking her head for emphasis. "Not this time."

"What did the person look like?" asked Mr. Gracie, listening closely as he always did.

"I didn't see the face," said Sarah, a bit calmer now, "but he or she was dressed in white."

"Like a ghost?" said Eliza, nudging William. "Maybe it was the ghost of Mrs. Walton."

"I'm not making this up, Eliza!" Sarah said. "I admit I made up the stories about the singing roses and the broom made of human hair, but this time I really *saw* someone! Maybe it *was* a ghost!"

Mr. and Mrs. Gracie looked at each other in bewilderment.

"I'll ask Henry to search the house and the grounds," Mr. Gracie said. "Would that make you feel better, Sarah?"

Sarah nodded. "But can I sleep in Eliza's room tonight? I really think it was Mrs. Walton's ghost."

"That's not fair," said Eliza. "This is supposed to be my first night alone in my new room. I've been waiting for this day all my life."

"What's more important, Eliza, your room or your sister?" asked Mrs. Gracie, not expecting an answer.

"Fine," Eliza said quietly. "You can sleep in my room."

"Maybe someone came in through the secret underground passageway," said Archie.

"I don't think we have to worry about that," said Mr. Gracie. "That door is so well hidden that the carpenters never even found it."

"Well, I'm not going to go exploring down in the basement," said Sarah. "I'd rather be upstairs where everyone can hear me if I have to scream again."

"Hopefully that won't happen," said Mr. Gracie.

"I want to go find the secret passage," said Archie. "Can I go down to the basement now, Papa?"

"Absolutely not," Mrs. Gracie answered for her husband. "I don't want anyone going down to the basement until Henry has looked around. And any-way, Archie, where did you disappear to before?"

"I was hiding in a tree," said Archie. "William found me. I'm a pretty good climber, aren't I William?"

"You will be if you remember you have to climb down again," William said, smiling. "How about helping Papa and me unload the wagon?"

"That's a good idea," said Mr. Gracie. "I don't want you wandering around near the river either, Archie. That goes for all of you—unless you're with me. As I said before, this part of the river can be very dangerous."

ONCE THEY FINISHED UNLOADING the wagon and carrying the trunks and parcels into the front hall, Mr. Gracie took William, Eliza, Sarah, and Mrs. Gracie on a tour of the upstairs. First they went into the nursery where Lizzie was unpacking a cloth bag of baby clothes. She was to sleep in a small room adjoining the nursery. Lizzie made sure that the young ones were playing quietly in a corner before joining the Gracies on their tour of the upstairs.

The upstairs hallway was wide with four doors opening onto it. "This is Archie's room," said Mr. Gracie, opening a door. Archie walked in, looked around quickly, and turned toward William. "Will you visit me here?" he hoped. William nodded. "Then I like it," Archie said, smiling.

Next, Mr. Gracie showed them Eliza's room, and then William's room, which was at the far end of the hall. As soon as William looked inside, he knew why his father had chosen it for him. It had the best view of the river. He saw a sleek vessel sailing by in the dusk. Since he was higher up than the study, he could see the bathing pavilion between the dock and the beach by the cove.

Next, Mr. Gracie led them to a room on the other side of the hall. "This is Sarah's room," he said. The others peered inside.

"It's nice, Sarah," said Eliza. She pointed to a miniature leather chair opposite the bed. "That's the perfect place for what's her name—your china doll?"

"Rebecca Anne," said Sarah, "and I *said* I'm not sleeping here alone. Don't try to convince me otherwise. I'll bring the little chair into your room so Rebecca Anne can watch us both sleep."

"I thought you wanted your own room so you could feel like a princess," said Lizzie. "Why do you want to sleep in Eliza's room?"

Thud! The sudden sound came from downstairs.

"That's why," said Sarah, grabbing Lizzie's arm. "There's someone in this house!"

"Who's there?" Mr. Gracie shouted, hurrying down the stairs. When he got no answer, he looked at Mrs. Gracie. "You stay upstairs with Archie and the girls while William and I check the first floor and basement. If there is an intruder, we're going to find him."

"*Her,*" Sarah corrected him, grasping Lizzie's hand. "I don't think Mrs. Walton's ghost wants us here."

"Oh, Sarah," said Mrs. Gracie, trying hard to remain calm. "This is not the time to be telling stories. Maybe something fell."

As William followed his father down the stairs, he wondered if Sarah really had seen someone. And, if she had, what would that person want from the Gracie family?

5

THE NEXT MORNING, WILLIAM AROSE AT THE crack of dawn. He felt such a thrill of waking up in a new bedroom with a view of the sun rising over the East River that he hardly missed the city noises at all. Quickly, he washed and dressed, and then joined his father in the dining room for an early breakfast. It wasn't until Lizzie served them bowls of oatmeal that William remembered the strange events of the day before. After they had heard the *thud*, he and his father had searched the first floor and basement of the house, as well as the property that surrounded it. They hadn't found anyone. Neither had Henry Fellows when he looked that night.

"Do you think Sarah made up the story of seeing someone going down to the kitchen?" William asked his father, looking around for the sugar bowl.

"She could have," said Mr. Gracie. "After all, your sister does have a vivid imagination."

"But Mr. Gracie," said Lizzie, "what about the *thud* we all heard?" said Lizzie. She was folding a napkin as she stood in the entryway of the dining room. Aside from the three of them, everyone else was asleep.

"Something could have fallen," said William. He got up and walked toward the door that led downstairs to the kitchen. "Maybe one of the trunks turned on its side and we didn't notice when we were carrying them up to the rooms."

"What are you looking for?" Lizzie asked, following him toward the cellar door.

"The sugar," said William.

"I must have forgotten to put it on the table," said Lizzie as she and William walked down the stairs single file. "I haven't gotten a chance to unpack everything we brought from the city. I had to mind Robert and Hettie all afternoon. Let me see . . . the sugar should be in a trunk labeled *Provisions*—over in that corner."

William went over to a stack of three trunks in the corner Lizzie had pointed to. One, which Lizzie had already unpacked, was labeled *Linens*. The other two were labeled *Plates* and *Silverware*. "The provisions trunk isn't here," said William.

"Well, I know we brought it," said Lizzie, looking puzzled. "I saw it yesterday in the front hall."

Just then Mr. Gracie came down to the kitchen, as well. "Maybe it's in another room, William," he said. "Can you do without it for now? We have a long day of work ahead of us."

"Yes, Papa," said William, feeling confused. He could have sworn he'd brought four trunks down the cellar steps and into the kitchen himself the day before. He and Mr. Gracie went back upstairs where William quickly finished the oatmeal, bland without the sugar, before joining his father in their new study a few minutes later.

By the time the rest of the family woke up, William and Mr. Gracie were hard at work. They spent all morning unpacking and organizing timetables, reports, and correspondence that had been transported from the Broadway house. William felt a bit overwhelmed by the complexity of having to keep track of so many arriving and departing ships and the lengthiness of some of the cargo lists. With all the challenging work ahead of him, he was grateful that his father was patient while explaining things. As the morning wore on, Mr. Gracie made a pile of papers he wanted William to read. The stack was over a foot high by the time they joined the rest of the family for lunch on the porch.

William was relieved to relax in the warm, open air. He was hungry and tired and, after hearing about the activities of his brothers and sisters on their first morning at Horn's Hook, wished he could take the rest of the afternoon off. He scolded himself for even thinking such a thing. *I'm not a child anymore*, he thought.

As they sat around the table, everyone seemed to be talking at once. The weather couldn't have been more perfect. Eliza and Sarah had helped Henry Fellows clear a small garden plot so they could grow vegetables outside one of the half-windows of the kitchen.

"This afternoon, Mama and I are going to plant lettuce, cucumber, tomatoes, and corn," said Eliza.

"What about watermelon?" Archie wondered. "That's what I want to grow."

"We don't have any watermelon seeds today," said Mrs. Gracie. "But we can ask Henry to get some for us."

"Okay," said Archie, biting into his third biscuit.

"Sarah, aren't you going to help in the garden?" William asked.

"I've had enough gardening for one day," said Sarah. "I'm going to sit out on the lawn and read."

"Why don't you sit on the porch?" offered William. "You'll be more comfortable and have a better view."

"I'm not going to sit on the porch by myself," said Sarah. "What if the ghost comes back?"

"There are no such thing as ghosts," said Eliza. "Papa and William looked everywhere and couldn't find anything suspicious. Neither did Henry Fellows when he looked last night."

"Look, Eliza," said Sarah. "Ghosts can make themselves invisible when they want to. I know a ghost when I see one. I also know a noise when I hear one. I know you didn't see what I saw, but you certainly heard what I heard. Why is it so hard for you and everyone else to believe that Mrs. Walton's ghost is hanging around our house which was built on the foundation of her's?"

"I guess you must be right," said Eliza, winking at William.

But William didn't wink back. Instead, he made a mental note to look for the absent provisions trunk that was missing from the kitchen.

"Guess where Lizzie took me, Robert, and Hettie this morning," Archie said to William.

"To England," said William, teasing his younger brother.

"No," William giggled. "To the beach at the cove. I went in up to my ankles and caught a glass full of minnows. Robert stuck his hand in it and tried to eat them."

William smiled. "Wasn't the water cold?" he asked.

"Freezing," said Archie. "But I went in anyway. Did you have fun working?"

"We were too busy to have fun," said William. "But I'm learning so much about what Papa does. We have some very important matters to take care of."

"Wouldn't you rather be outside playing?" asked Sarah, helping herself to more peas.

"No," said William. "I'm a little old for that."

"Nonsense," said Mr. Gracie. "You'll have plenty of time for relaxing on Sunday afternoons. Don't make the mistake of growing up too fast."

William was secretly pleased and relieved that he'd have some free time—even if it was only on Sunday afternoons. On Sunday mornings, Mrs. Gracie would be giving the children bible lessons since the closest church was far away.

After lunch, William and Mr. Gracie returned to their cool study which was only beginning to look organized. While William was examining a cargo list, there was a knock on the door.

"Come in," called Mr. Gracie.

Lizzie walked into the room with Hettie on her hip and handed Mr. Gracie a letter. "This was just delivered from New York City," she said, and left.

William watched as his father opened the letter. "Who's it from?" he asked.

"My business associate, Mr. Wolcott," said Mr. Gracie. "It's a copy of the letter that was sent to all the captains of our ships." He handed the letter to William who read aloud:

Direct your vessels to stop in the Cove, below Hell Gate, south of General Stevens' house, with direction to have your letters left at Mr. Gracie's house on the opposite side of the river. The hands will thereby be safe and some detention avoided.

It was signed by Mr. Wolcott.

"I hope you're not still worried that there won't be enough to do here at Horn's Hook," said Mr. Gracie, handing William a document marked IMPORTANT.

"Not one bit," William said. "What's this?"

"You tell me," said Mr. Gracie.

"William studied the sheet of paper for a moment. "It's a cargo list," he said. "For the *Virginia*, the ship that's due to arrive . . . let me see. Oh . . . here it is. It should be arriving sometime next month."

"You're learning quickly, William," said Mr. Gracie. With the unpredictability of tides and winds, we can't be more precise than that. I'd like you to check next month's timetables for arriving and departing ships and make sure the *Virginia* has a place to dock in New York Harbor. The *Virginia* is one of our most important ships."

William liked the way his father said *our most important ships*. It made him feel as if he and his father were partners. He looked forward to the arrival of the *Virginia*—especially since it would be the first of their ships to stop at Horn's Hook.

"I'd like you to copy the cargo list over on a fresh sheet of parchment," Mr. Gracie said, holding up an old cargo list on which the printing was flawless. "It must be letter perfect like this one. I'd like three copies."

"Yes, Papa," William said, taking some parchment from the top drawer of his desk. He dipped his quill in an inkwell and began to write.

Making a "letter perfect" copy of the *Virginia's* cargo list was harder work than William had expected. He had to start over three times before he got halfway through. *But I enjoy hard work*, he reminded himself.

Finally, just before dusk, Mr. Gracie looked up from his papers. "Why don't you go get some fresh air with your brothers and sisters," he said to William.

"Are you quitting too?" William asked his father.

"I still have a few more things to do," said Mr. Gracie. "I'll work until supper."

"Then I'll stay and work as well," said William. Though he wanted to go outside more than anything, he wanted his father to know how serious he was about his work.

"Suit yourself," said Mr. Gracie, returning to his papers.

THAT NIGHT AT DINNER, MRS. Gracie read aloud a note she'd received from Aunt Elizabeth the day before, welcoming the Gracies to their new country home.

"It says they wanted to be here when we arrived, but David had to return to the city for some business," said Mrs. Gracie. "I sent a return note inviting them to spend the first Sunday afternoon in June here at Horn's Hook. I've asked your uncles Nehemiah, Moses, and Henry as well." Nehemiah, Moses, and Henry, Mrs. Gracie's brothers, had large families as well.

"Do you think they'll come?" asked Sarah.

"I know Aunt Elizabeth will probably come," said Mrs. Gracie. "But the others might not because they haven't left the city yet."

William noticed that Eliza looked a bit nervous. "Don't worry," he said, unable to resist teasing his sister, "James will be here."

"That's *not* why I asked," said Eliza. "It's just that it's only a week away. I hope Lizzie can find the time to put my hair up."

Just then, Lizzie came into the dining room looking puzzled.

"What's wrong?" Mrs. Gracie asked her.

"The strangest thing happened," Lizzie said. "I was up in the nursery putting Robert and Hettie to bed. When I came back down to the kitchen, the trunk I had been missing this morning was sitting in the corner—the one labeled *Provisions*. I opened it and found that every item was there, but half the amounts were missing.

6

"**I**T SOUNDS AS IF SOMEONE PLAYED A TRICK ON you, Lizzie," said Mr. Gracie, looking around at his children. "Who hid the trunk from Lizzie?"

"Why are you looking at me?" said Archie. "I always get blamed for everything."

"I don't mean to accuse anyone," said Mr. Gracie, "but I must get to the bottom of this. Did you do it, Archie?" Mr. Gracie looked frustrated.

"The trunk would have been too heavy for Archie to lift," said Lizzie.

"Maybe Eliza did it," said Sarah. "Just to scare me." Everyone's eyes turned toward Eliza.

"That's not fair!" Eliza said, defensively. "I know I tease Sarah sometimes, but I have better things to do than to steal from Lizzie."

William knew he would never understand the complex relationship between his sisters. Sometimes they acted like the best of friends, other times like the worst of enemies.

"Anyway," said Eliza, "if I did decide to play a joke, I'd probably sneak up on you in the middle of the night and wake you out of a sound sleep. Maybe someone's come through the secret underground passageway in the basement."

"I'll go down and look for it first thing tomorrow morning," said William.

"I don't want anyone going down to the basement," said Mrs. Gracie. "That includes you, William. I know it's very unlikely that anyone knows about the secret passageway, but I just won't feel comfortable knowing you're poking around in the dark."

"But I'll go with him," Archie pleaded.

"No you won't," said Mr. Gracie. "The last thing we want to do is worry your mother."

"Has anyone thought of asking William about the trunk?" asked Eliza. "Maybe he took it." Everyone looked at William.

"I'm the one who discovered that it was missing in the first place," William said. "You might as well ask Robert and Hettie. Or maybe Henry Fellows is the culprit."

There was a sudden silence as everyone thought about the possibility.

"Haven't you ever read a book?" said Sarah, looking at each of the Gracies. "Someone like Henry Fellows is the obvious person to blame, but he's never the one who actually commits the crime. It's always the ghost—in this case, Mrs. Walton's ghost. Can't you see that Mrs. Walton's ghost wants to live here in peace? You have no idea of the horrible things she can do to get rid of us."

"Sarah," said Mr. Gracie. "I really don't think you have anything to be afraid of. We're not going back to the city. Thousands of people have died from the yellow fever epidemic in the last six years. I am intent on staying here. But until we find out what's been going on, I don't want anyone to wander around alone. I'll ask Henry Fellows, though I was introduced to him several years ago by a respectable sea captain and have always known him to be honest."

"Listen to your father," said Mrs. Gracie to everyone. "Don't go anywhere alone."

WHEN MR. GRACIE ASKED HENRY Fellows if he knew anything about the trunk that disappeared and reappeared he was just as perplexed as the rest of the family. "We just have to hope that this doesn't happen again," said Mr. Gracie.

There has to be a good explanation for all of this, thought William. *But what? And with all the work he had to do, when would he find time to figure out what it was?*

The rest of the week went by quickly. At first, the Gracie children were very careful about not going anywhere alone—whether they were in the garden, down at the cove, at the stables, inside the house— even on the porch.

During that time, the only thing they couldn't find was Eliza's grammar book. She had agreed to bring it along to make up for the school work she'd missed when she was sick for two weeks the winter before. Everyone knew she hadn't wanted to bring it. While grammar was Sarah's best subject, it was Eliza's worst.

"You probably left it at home on purpose,"

Archie had said. "Without it you'll have more time for your needlepoint."

But Eliza insisted that she remembered unpacking the grammar book and putting it on a small table in her room. When she asked Sarah if she had seen it, Sarah said, "No, but I wouldn't be surprised if Mrs. Walton's ghost wants to brush up on her grammar."

Archie was still sleeping in his own room despite Mrs. Gracie's urging him to sleep in William's. He insisted that he was a big boy like William now.

WILLIAM FOUND THAT WORKING FOR his father was more challenging than he could have imagined. He remembered a clerk from the city had once told him that working for Mr. Gracie taught him more than he could learn after four years at Columbia College. William now knew what he meant.

The most exciting part of the job was watching the ships sail through Hell Gate. The foaming waves rose several feet high and the captains and crew members, at least from what William could sense, looked intensely focused. Once they'd gone through it safely, they seemed to relax. He couldn't wait for the *Virginia* to arrive.

William spent most of his time copying over the cargo lists of the *Virginia* and familiarizing himself with the details of its expected arrival. His father told him to make a note whenever he couldn't decipher what was written, and ask the captain about it when the ship arrived. Every so often when he looked out the window and saw Archie climbing a tree or heard his mother in the garden, he wished he were outside with them. But instead of complaining, he moved his gaze to the ships and reminded himself that he had a job to do.

AS PLANNED, THE LAMBERT FAMILY arrived at noon on the first Monday in June. The Rogers cousins wouldn't be able to join them until later in the summer when they came to stay with the Lamberts. The warm, sunny weather inspired everyone to spend the afternoon at the cove where the water was finally warming up.

Mr. and Mrs. Gracie and Mr. and Mrs. Lambert sat under two large umbrellas on the grass with the younger children while the older children waded in the water, digging in the mud with small shellfish rakes for clams and oysters. Lizzie was up at the house taking a few hours off.

William enjoyed spending time with cousin James who was only a year younger than he was. Charlotte Lambert was a year older than Sarah, and Thomas was the same age as Archie.

William noticed that Eliza, for the first time in her life, was acting shy. He wondered if James noticed the difference in her.

"I found a clam!" Archie shouted, holding up his treasure. Everyone looked and applauded the first time but after a while finding shellfish became routine.

"How come Eliza's so much quieter than usual?" James asked William when they were a good distance from the others.

William shrugged. "I can never figure her out."

"I have an idea," said James with a mischievous look in his eye. He waded toward Eliza, whose back was to him, and splashed her from behind.

Eliza spun around furiously. "My hair!" she cried,

miserably. Lizzie had spent two hours fixing it the night before.

"I'm sorry," said James, turning red. "Really, I am. I thought you'd start laughing."

Suddenly, Eliza blushed. "I forgive you," she said, "but I'm getting out." With wet dripping hair, she walked toward the shore. For the rest of the afternoon, she sat on the shore with her needlepoint.

By three o'clock, they had filled two large nets with over sixty clams and oysters. After rinsing off at the bathing pavilion, William and James brought the filled nets to the house so Lizzie could prepare them for dinner. Archie took Thomas to his favorite tree, determined not to get stuck. Eliza joined Sarah and Charlotte under a maple tree where they talked about what had happened since they'd last seen each other. Finally Lizzie called them in for supper.

Never had any of the Gracies or Lamberts tasted clams or oysters as delicious as those Lizzie had prepared. Everything else was appetizing as well— the roast Henry had bought downtown from the butcher the day before, cooked vegetables, and many different relishes.

"What a perfect day," said Sarah. Everyone agreed.

As William watched the sky grow dark, listened to the songs of chirping crickets, and felt the cool breeze from the river, he was overwhelmed by a feeling of happiness. *I really don't miss New York City at all*, he thought contentedly.

Eliza sat across from him, seemingly more

relaxed than she'd been earlier. Needlepoint always made her feel peaceful. She was deep in conversation with James who sat next to her. William could tell that James admired Eliza as much as Eliza admired him—though she'd never admit it. William hoped that one day he'd meet a young lady he cared about.

"Archibald, Esther, we'd like you to come to a party next Saturday evening," Aunt Elizabeth said, smiling.

"I love parties," Sarah said.

"Sarah!" Mrs. Gracie said. "Your aunt wasn't talking to you."

"Actually, Sarah, this party is just for grown-ups," Aunt Elizabeth said kindly. Then she turned back to Mrs. Gracie. "We've invited the Beekmans, the Joneses, the Schemerhorns, and several other families with summer houses around the area. Nehemiah and his family may even come up from the city. We've hired violinists. It will be a late-night affair."

"We'd love to come," Mrs. Gracie said, looking at her agreeable husband.

"Sarah, did you help your mother and Eliza plant those beautiful marigolds in your vegetable garden?" asked Aunt Elizabeth, noticing Sarah's disappointment over not being on the guest list.

Sarah nodded. "It was my idea. I think they look like soldiers protecting the lettuces, don't you?" She looked relieved to be included in the conversation again.

"I never thought of them like that," Aunt

Elizabeth said, laughing.

"Let's hope those marigolds are the only soldiers we see," said Mr. Gracie.

"What do you mean, Papa?" William asked, hoping Lizzie would bring out dessert soon.

"The English and the French are at war with each other now. Their disagreements are having an effect on American shipping."

"In what way?" asked James, turning away from Eliza.

"President Jefferson feels that the only way to keep us out of the war is for us to remain neutral. This would mean we'd have to stop shipping goods to both countries."

"Do you agree with President Jefferson?" asked Mr. Lambert, putting down his fork.

"No, I disagree," said Mr. Gracie. "I believe we should continue shipping to both countries. After all, we still have our ministers there. Both of them are not only business associates of mine but good friends as well. Alexander Hamilton is coming soon to go over the legal matters with me, but it's very likely that we'll continue trading as usual. If we follow President Jefferson's policy, it can only lead to disaster for American shipping merchants."

Suddenly, Lizzie came out empty-handed and looking upset.

"What's the matter, Lizzie?" said Mrs. Gracie. "Where's our dessert?"

With bewilderment, Lizzie exclaimed, "The sugar wafers I made this afternoon are gone!"

7

"**T**HE GHOST TOOK IT!" SARAH EXCLAIMED. "The ghost took the sugar wafers!"

"Ghost?" asked Charlotte.

"What's this nonsense about a ghost?" asked Aunt Elizabeth, looking from Mr. Gracie to Mrs. Gracie. William noticed the embarrassment on his parents' faces.

"Of course we don't believe there's a ghost," said Mrs. Gracie.

"Then who borrowed the provisions trunk?" asked Archie. "And who did Sarah see going down to the kitchen?"

"What's been going on around here?" said Mr. Lambert, looking concerned.

William spoke before his parents had a chance. "Ever since we arrived, things have been missing," he said. "Sarah thought she saw someone lurking around the kitchen. A trunk of provisions was taken from the kitchen and then returned only half full. And now, we're going to have to do without dessert."

"Esther and I were going to ask you if you've heard about any intruders in the area," said Mr. Gracie, "but it's been such an enjoyable day, I honestly forgot to bring it up."

William noticed James turning to Eliza. "Do you believe in ghosts?" he inquired so only she could hear.

"Of course not," Eliza said, rolling her eyes. "Sarah walks around with her head in the clouds most of the time."

"I do not," said Sarah, "and you know it. How do you explain your missing grammar book?"

Eliza shrugged. "Maybe there is an intruder," she said, "but if there is, it's a person."

"There must be a good explanation for all this," James said, knitting his brows.

"There is," said Sarah. "The ghost of Mrs. Walton stole Lizzie's sugar wafers hoping she'd make all of us mad enough to leave so she could have the house to herself."

"Who is Mrs. Walton?" asked Thomas, wanting to be part of the adult conversation.

"The lady who lived on this property before we did," William explained. "Our house was built on the same foundation as her house."

"She loved her house so much she called it her 'fair heart's desire'," said Sarah. "And she cried when she had to leave it. Now she's haunting it."

"Enough, Sarah," warned Mrs. Gracie. "There are no such thing as ghosts."

"I've got it!" said Aunt Elizabeth. Everyone turned toward her with interest. "Something similar happened to us last summer. Our neighbors brought over a basket of sugar plums and an hour later they were missing."

"Did you ever find them?" asked Archie.

"No," said Aunt Elizabeth, "because someone ate them. A little boy we all know." She was looking directly at Thomas.

"I couldn't help myself," Thomas said, trying to defend himself. "But I learned my lesson. My stomach ached for two days and I had to stay indoors for three."

Archie giggled.

"Do you mean you think one of our children ate enough wafers for a dozen people?" asked Mrs. Gracie, looking offended.

"Well," said Aunt Elizabeth. "Maybe one of ours did it—though I hope not. Not counting Robert and Hettie, there are seven children here today." William didn't like being called a child but didn't want to be rude and interrupt his aunt. "Each of them was in the house at some point. I know Thomas and Archie came up to the house to get nets. William and James brought the clams and oysters up. Even Sarah brought Charlotte up to the house to show her Rebecca Anne."

"Who?" asked James, looking puzzled.

"Rebecca Anne," said Charlotte, as if he should have known. "Sarah's china doll."

"I see," James said, trying to keep a serious face.

"And Eliza came up to get her needlepoint!" said Lizzie, suddenly looking hopeful. "Which one of you children ate my sugar wafers?"

"Not me."

"I didn't do it."

"We didn't even go into the kitchen."

Like the others, William denied stealing the sugar wafers. Considering their children honest, Mr.

and Mrs. Gracie and Mr. and Mrs. Lambert had no other thoughts on the subject. That night, the Gracies bolted all the doors and windows, and the missing sugar wafers remained a mystery.

AS EXPECTED, THE *VIRGINIA* CAME into view about a week later. William was the first to see it through the window in front of his desk. With great enthusiasm, he grabbed his father's telescope and rushed out to the porch where Mrs. Gracie sat knitting. Archie was swaying on a wooden swing that Henry Fellows had hung from a cherry tree next to the porch.

"Well, look at that," said Mrs. Gracie, putting down her needlework. "Eliza! Sarah!" she called down to the kitchen where Lizzie was showing the two girls how to make a perfect pie crust. "Come see Papa's ship." Eliza and Sarah hurried upstairs and onto the porch. "It's the first one to stop at Horn's Hook."

"Where's it coming from?" asked Archie.

"England," said William, looking through the telescope. "It should be here in less than twenty minutes. "He handed the telescope to Eliza, wondering where his father had gone.

"It's beautiful!" said Eliza, looking through the narrow cylinder. She handed the telescope to Sarah.

"I wonder if there are pirates on it?" said Sarah.

"I want to see! I want to see!" said Archie, rushing toward the others. Sarah handed him the telescope and showed him how to use it.

"It's so big!" said Archie, still looking through the telescope. "Boy, there sure are a lot of ships out today."

It was true. They could see several ships farther away than the *Virginia* and several that were closer. One vessel had just entered Hell Gate, with foaming waves breaking on both sides of its hull.

"I must go find Papa," William said, as soon as he could make out the name of the *Virginia*. "He'll want to be here when it arrives."

"He told me he was going over to the stables this morning to feed the horses," said Mrs. Gracie. "Henry's feeling a bit under the weather. Perhaps he's still there."

William ran toward the stables, excited to tell his father that he'd spotted the *Virginia*. When he was halfway there, he saw his father waving at him and pointing toward the ship."

I should have known he'd have already seen it, William thought. *Nothing escapes my father's eyes.*

William and Mr. Gracie led the others down toward the docks to meet John Stewart, the captain of the *Virginia*. As soon as the ship sailed through the turbulent current of Hell Gate and into the calmer waters near Horn's Hook, they all cheered the skilled captain. Captain Stewart and the crew waved.

The Gracies watched the sailors lower a small rowboat over the side of the *Virginia*. As soon as it was in the water, a sailor rowed the captain ashore and tied the boat to a wooden post at the dock near the bathing pavilion.

"Your arrival couldn't be more timely," Mr. Gracie said to the captain as he stepped onto the wooden dock. "My son William and I have worked out most of the arrangements for the rest of your trip." He gestured toward William making him feel very important.

"It's a great pleasure to meet you, Sir," William said, shaking hands with the captain. "I've been working on the cargo lists for your ship and, when we have a few moments, I have some questions."

"I'd be happy to help you in any way I can," said Captain Stewart.

Mr. Gracie gave William a look of approval and then said to the captain, "I am expecting my business associate and lawyer to arrive in a day or two with the final information."

"That's good news," said Captain Stewart. "I'm looking forward to journeying around the Cape of Good Hope to Madras and Calcutta. I've heard that our goods are highly desired there."

"The English and the French want those Spanish coins you're transporting," replied Mr. Gracie. "The trip will be very worthwhile."

"Wonderful," said the captain, looking around at the rest of the Gracies.

"I'd like you to meet my wife, Esther, my daughters, Eliza and Sarah, and my other son Archie," Mr. Gracie said proudly. Everyone greeted the captain.

"Would you like some tea on the porch?" asked Lizzie, walking toward them.

"And this is Lizzie," said Mr. Gracie.

"What a nice family," said the captain. "I'd love a cup of tea.

Mr. Gracie, William, and Captain Stewart spent the next few hours discussing business on the porch. Thrilled to sit in on his first business meeting, William thought carefully before he said anything, hoping not to utter the wrong thing.

"I'm going to see how Henry Fellows, our caretaker, is doing," Mr. Gracie said, taking William by surprise. He hadn't expected to carry on the meeting by himself. "William, why don't you get the *Virginia*'s cargo list and go over your questions with Captain Stewart."

"Yes, Sir," William said, proud that his father was trusting him to finish up the meeting. He went toward the small parlor study to get the cargo list, some parchment, and his quill, which he'd left neatly on top of his desk. But when he opened the door, all he saw was the cargo list. The pile of blank paper and quill weren't where he had left them.

Maybe Archie took them, he thought, planning to scold his little brother for snooping where he didn't belong.

He looked all over: on top of his desk, inside it, and even on his father's. But there was no sign of either one. *I mustn't keep the captain waiting*, he thought, wishing he had time to search longer. Instead, he borrowed his father's pen, carefully slid another piece of parchment from the desk, and returned to the porch to clarify certain items on the cargo list.

The rest of the meeting went well. Captain Stewart was very helpful and gave William the information he needed to complete the new list. Mr. Gracie returned an hour later, just before the captain was ready to row back to the anchored *Virginia*.

"We'll raise a blue flag above the porch to let you know when Alexander Hamilton has arrived," Mr. Gracie said to the captain. "It shouldn't be more than a few days." Then he walked Captain Stewart down to where his rowboat was waiting.

William watched from the porch as his father and the captain finished up their conversation next to the bathing pavilion near the water. Finally the captain returned to the rowboat. A member of his crew promptly rowed him back to the ship.

As soon as the captain had gone, Mr. Gracie came up to the house and complimented William on a job well done. William couldn't remember ever having felt as proud as he did that day.

After dinner that night, William went to Archie's room and scolded him for taking the quill and parchment.

"What quill and parchment?" Archie wondered. "I didn't take anything."

"Are you sure?" William said.

"Yes, I'm sure." Archie looked hurt.

"Well, someone took them," William said uneasily. "And I'm sorry I thought it was you." He'd known his brother long enough to know he was telling the truth.

"Maybe it was the ghost," said Archie. "I know you don't believe in ghosts, but Sarah does."

"Sarah does what?" asked Sarah, joining them in the hall.

While Archie told Sarah what had happened, Eliza met them in the hall.

"Let's all go into my room so Mama and Papa don't hear us," said William, suddenly remembering the spot where his father and Captain Stewart had been talking. "I have a plan."

8

EARLY SATURDAY EVENING, AFTER MR. AND MRS. Gracie set off in a carriage for the Lamberts' party, William, Eliza, Sarah, and Archie tiptoed down the rickety basement steps. For the past two days, none of them had been able to think about anything except for William's plan to find the secret underground passage. Twice, Mr. Gracie had caught William lost in thought as he gazed out the window. "What are you thinking about?" he had asked.

"Nothing, Papa," William had said with embarrassment. "I didn't sleep very well."

"It smells kind of damp down here!" said Archie. The basement was cool with a low ceiling and a paved brick floor. Though the cellar was fairly bright from the half windows on the surrounding walls, William carried a lantern.

"Shh," said Sarah. "What if Lizzie hears us?"

"She won't," said Eliza. "She went down to the cove with the little ones. I reminded her how much fun they always have there."

"Good thinking," said William. Though Lizzie could usually be depended on to keep a secret, he didn't want to take any chances. Mr. and Mrs. Gracie had forbid their children to go exploring in the basement and here they were, breaking a rule.

"I hope we find the ghost in the secret passage-way," said Archie.

"I don't," said Sarah, reaching the bottom step. "In fact, I don't think we should be doing this at all. Archie is right. It smells musty down here."

"Oh, Sarah," said Eliza. "please, we need all the help we can get."

"Okay," said Sarah, "but we'll be sorry. Boy, it sure is dusty."

"Yeah," said Archie. "And why is it so cold down here?"

Ignoring all of the complaints, William hung a lantern from one of the rafters so it lit up more of the room. "Now we can see even better"

"Do you have any idea where we're supposed to look for this secret passage?" Eliza asked William.

"How can he?" said Sarah. "Even Papa doesn't know."

"Actually, I have a pretty good idea about where it is," William explained as the others stared at him. "Do you remember where Papa and the captain of the *Virginia* were standing the other day?"

"Down by the bathing pavilion?" said Archie.

"Exactly," said William. "Directly below our house—at the spot closest to the river."

"I'm not following you," said Sarah.

"When the Waltons lived here they had to travel everywhere by water since there were few passable roads," William explained carefully. "So they'd probably build the passageway as close to the river as possible."

"I see!" said Eliza, her eyes lighting up. "They'd build it from the basement to the place Papa and Captain Stewart were standing. From there, they could jump in a boat and escape." William nodded.

"So how do we find the entrance?" asked Sarah, looking in the dimness at the stone wall. The dock and the bathing pavilion were on the other side.

"I think we should run our hands along every spot in this entire wall, looking for strange bumps," said William. "Let's start right near the wine cellar."

"We could also knock," said Sarah, suddenly seeming interested. "I just remembered a story Charlotte told me last summer. It was really scary. It took place in an old, haunted town where . . . "

"Get to the point, Sarah," Eliza said, trying not to sound insulting.

"The two boys in the story were looking for a hidden door, so they knocked on the walls," Sarah said. "They finally found the door in a place that sounded hollow."

"Thanks, Sarah," said William, "that's a great idea." The others agreed. They walked over to the wall which was dim in the lantern light.

"I can't reach the top part of the wall," Archie complained.

"Actually, that's a good thing, Archie," William said. "Your job is to check the part that is closest to the floor. Sarah and Eliza can check the middle part, and I'll check the top. We'll use our different sizes to our best advantage."

"Let's start already," said Sarah, walking to one

end of the wall. "I don't want to be down here longer than I have to." She began to knock. Eliza and William started on the other end of the wall, and Archie insisted on starting in the middle.

For the next few minutes, everything was silent except for the knocking. Suddenly, a voice said, "Who's there?"

Stunned, all four Gracies froze in place.

"I said, 'Who's there? Who's in that basement.'"

"That's Lizzie," William whispered, relaxing a little. "What should we say."

"I know you're down there!" Lizzie warned in a shaky voice. "I'm going to lock the door until the master of the house returns!"

"We have to tell her it's us," whispered Eliza. "Otherwise she'll tell Mama and Papa that she heard someone roaming around down here. She'll also wonder where we are."

They heard the door at the top of the stairs slam.

"Lizzie! It's us!" They yelled as loud as they could.

The door opened. "William? Eliza? Is that you?"

"It's Archie and me, too!" yelled Sarah. "Please don't lock us in. It's cold and dark down here."

"Come upstairs at once," said Lizzie. "I want to know what's going on."

William led the others upstairs. They squinted in the dining room light as Lizzie stared at them. Robert and Hettie were playing on the floor.

"What in the world were you doing down there?" asked Lizzie. "You know you're not allowed . . . "

"We thought you were at the cove with Robert and Hettie," said William.

"I was," said Lizzie, "until it started raining." As if on cue, a crash of thunder sounded, followed by lightning.

"We hadn't even noticed," said Sarah. "We were so busy knocking on the walls, looking for the hidden door."

"We're sorry, Lizzie," William said. "We didn't mean to scare you, but we have to find that secret underground passage. Someone has been coming into this house and we want to find out who it is."

"Please don't tell Mama and Papa," Eliza begged.

"I won't," Lizzie said, surprising everybody. As much as Lizzie loved the children, she rarely kept anything from Mr. and Mrs. Gracie. "You're right, we have to find out who's been taking things. Before I took the little ones down to the cove, I went to get the blue and white blanket from the closet. But it wasn't there."

"This is really getting spooky," said Sarah. "Maybe we *shouldn't* be poking around down in the basement."

"I'm starting to agree with you, Sarah," Eliza said. "But we can't quit now."

Suddenly, Lizzie looked puzzled. "Has anyone seen Archie?"

"He was in the basement with us," said William, looking around the first floor of the house.

"I thought he came up with us," said Sarah.

"So did I," said Eliza. She opened the door to the

basement and called, "Archie!"

There was no answer.

"It's a good thing your parents will be out late," said Lizzie. "We must find Archie before they return. Let's go down to the basement and look. Sarah, can you stay with Robert and Hettie?"

"Sure," Sarah said in a shaky voice. "But hurry back. I don't like being the oldest one upstairs."

Sarah watched Robert and Hettie while Lizzie, William, and Eliza went back downstairs. "Archie!" they called. "Archie! Can you hear us?"

There was no answer.

9

THAT EVENING ROBERT AND HETTIE WERE THE only ones in the Gracie household who went to sleep at their normal bedtime. William, Eliza, and Sarah searched everywhere for Archie—in the basement, upstairs and downstairs, under the beds, behind the furniture, in the closets, the bathing pavilion, the stables, in all the climbing trees, and all around the grounds. Luckily the rain had turned into a light drizzle.

"I hope he didn't fall in the river," Eliza said, voicing the thought the others dreaded. The three of them were sitting in the front parlor in the darkness.

"Archie knows enough to stay away from the river," said William. "At least I hope he does."

"I told you we shouldn't have bothered Mrs. Walton's ghost," Sarah said, miserably. "Who do you think she'll take next?"

"Come now, Sarah," said William. "Ghosts are only in stories."

"And in secret passageways," said Eliza. "I'm beginning to think Sarah is right about the gh—"

"That's it!" cried William. "Follow me."

Sarah and Eliza followed their older brother into

the house, past the parlor, and back down into the basement.

"We already searched the basement," said Sarah.

"But we didn't search the secret passageway," said William. "Maybe Archie found it and got lost in it."

"How are we going to find Archie if we don't know where the secret passageway is?" Eliza asked, a look of doubt on her face.

"Well, we know Archie was feeling around and knocking on the lower part of the wall," said William, as he walked toward the wall. He bent down and started knocking. Eliza and Sarah joined him.

After a couple of minutes Sarah yelled, "I think I feel something! It sounds hollow when I knock. Come here! It's like a handle but it's kind of flat."

William and Eliza went over to Sarah and knelt beside her.

"You're right, Sarah," said William. "It does feel like a handle." He tugged on it, first one way, then the other. Nothing happened.

"Well, we know there was some sort of door here," said William. "Maybe if we all push on it when I count to three."

Eliza and Sarah placed their hands next to William's.

One, two, three . . . . They all pushed harder than they needed to. The low door opened into a dark passageway.

"We've found it!" Eliza said excitedly. "Let's get the lantern."

Eliza held the low door open while William

brought over the lantern from the rafter. As he held the lantern above the doorway, the three of them gasped. There, on the blue and white blanket that Lizzie was missing, lay Archie, with a tear-stained face, fast asleep.

"Archie! Wake up!" Sarah said, shaking her younger brother.

Archie sat up slowly, rubbing his eyes and looking confused. "You found me," he said, sniffling. "I thought I was lost forever."

"Oh, Archie, you scared us," said Eliza, unable to stifle back tears as she hugged her younger brother. "We thought we'd never find you."

"I'm so glad you're in one piece," Sarah said, also crying.

"Archie, you found the door to the secret underground passageway!" William said, also relieved to see his younger brother.

"I know," said Archie. "And I also met Mrs. Walton's ghost." His brother and sisters stared at him with disbelief.

"You *what?*" said Eliza.

"I met Mrs. Walton's ghost," said Archie, starting to feel more relaxed. "But she isn't a she. She's a he. And his name is Stefan."

Before they could question Archie further, Lizzie called down to them that their mother and father's carriage was coming up the drive.

10

THOUGH THEY HADN'T BEEN ABLE TO GET much sleep, William, Eliza, and Sarah woke up very early so they could meet at the stables as they had decided the night before. They planned to discuss what to do next. Luckily, the rain had stopped and the morning was cloudy with a warm breeze.

"I think one of us should explore the secret passageway," said William.

"I'm not going in there alone," said Sarah.

"I think two of us should go," said Eliza. "That way, if one of us is attacked, then the other one can run back for help."

"I don't think any of you should go." William, Eliza, and Sarah turned to find Lizzie coming toward them. She had been so happy to see Archie the night before that she picked him up and carried him to bed, despite his protests that he wasn't a baby anymore.

"But we have to, Lizzie," William said. "Papa is too busy to bother with this nonsense and we don't want Mama to keep worrying."

"Well, I don't want to see any one of you get hurt," said Lizzie. "You mean too much to me. I don't know what I would have done if we hadn't found Archie." She looked them each in the eye before heading back to the house to start breakfast. "Just be careful," she called out over her shoulder.

"We can't do anything until we talk to Archie," Eliza said. "We have to find out more about this man he saw."

"I agree," said William. "We'll talk to him after our bible lesson."

MR. AND MRS. GRACIE WOKE UP later than usual because they were out so late. As soon as the bible lesson concluded, breakfast was served. William, Eliza, and Sarah didn't get a chance to talk to Archie alone. They had breakfast in the dining room since some of the porch chairs were still wet from the storm the night before.

While they were eating, Mr. and Mrs. Gracie told them what a wonderful time they had at the Lamberts' party.

"I think James Lambert is enamored with you, Eliza," Mrs. Gracie said with a smile.

"That's nonsense," Eliza said, blushing. "What makes you think that?"

"He said he wished he could have invited you," Mr. Gracie said. "He needed a dancing partner."

"I thought it was only for grown-ups," said Sarah.

"It was," said Mrs. Gracie, "but James and Charlotte were there to greet the guests and James ended up staying for the first hour or so."

"Did you children have a nice evening without us?" Mr. Gracie asked, looking around the dining room table.

"It was nothing special, Papa," William said.

"Yes it was, William," Archie said, excitedly. "Tell Papa how I found the secret underground passageway and met the ghost.

"Ow!" Archie cried, when Eliza kicked him under the table. Then, seeing the look of disapproval on her face, he looked down at his plate. "Oops, I forgot we were supposed to keep it a secret."

"Didn't I tell you children that you weren't to go in the basement?" Mr. Gracie said sternly. He was looking right at William.

"I'm sorry, Papa," William said. "But we wanted to put an end to this mystery once and for all. I haven't had a chance to tell you that some parchment and my quill were missing from my desk."

"William thought I took them, but I didn't," Archie said, trying to get on his father's good side.

"I've always trusted you, William," Mr. Gracie said. William couldn't bear to meet his father's stare.

"It's not all William's fault," said Eliza. "Sarah and I went too."

"Did you know about this, Lizzie?" Mrs. Gracie asked. Lizzie stopped clearing the table and looked embarrassed.

"Lizzie told us not to do it," Sarah said.

William heard Lizzie sigh with relief.

"I'm torn between punishing you and wanting to know what you've found," said Mr. Gracie.

Just then, they heard a carriage pull up in front of the house.

"Are you expecting anybody?" Mrs. Gracie asked

Mr. Gracie.

"Not today," Mr. Gracie said with a shrug. "You know that I only work on Sundays when I have to. As do my business associates."

"I'll see who it is, Papa," William said, rising from his seat. He went through the hallway to the front door. Through the window he saw a man with red hair climbing down from a carriage with four horses.

"It's Mr. Hamilton!" William called back toward the dining room. Then he went outside to greet his father's friend with Mr. Gracie close behind him.

"Welcome, Alexander," Mr. Gracie called to the slight man with intense blue eyes. "Welcome to Horn's Hook—or I should say 'Gracie Mansion,' which my children have renamed it."

"What a nice piece of property you have," said Mr. Hamilton. "And the house is magnificent." He shook hands warmly with Mr. Gracie, and then William. The three of them walked toward the house.

"I'm sorry to bother you on a Sunday, but I have some business in Philadelphia and I wanted to take care of our matters first," said Mr. Hamilton.

William wasn't surprised that Mr. Hamilton's visit would be short. Alexander Hamilton always had business to take care of. He had once been a soldier with George Washington as well as the very first secretary of the treasury of the United States. He had also created the First Bank of the United States, an institution that allowed the country to grow and prosper by helping to repay debts they had incurred during the War for Independence.

William led him to the dining room where Lizzie had arranged an extra table setting at the head of the table. Before sitting down, Mr. Hamilton said hello to the other Gracies and apologized for interrupting their Sunday morning meal. Then, after rinsing his hands in a fresh bowl of water that Lizzie had provided, he sat down.

"There's no need to apologize," said Mrs. Gracie. "We're always happy to see you.

"I hope you're hungry," said Sarah, as Mr. Hamilton sat down. "The griddle cakes are very tasty."

"As a matter of fact, I am," said Mr. Hamilton, helping himself to a fresh peach that had been picked from one of the trees on the property. "Especially after such a long journey."

"Have you come from the city?" Eliza asked.

"Actually, I came from my new home in Harlem," Mr. Hamilton said, putting down his tea cup. "The bumps along the way were dreadful. Luckily it was a short ride. Do you think we ought to pave the roads, William?"

"I think it should be a very high priority," said William, pleased that the question had been directed toward him. "New York is an important city and we need to be able to travel around it more easily."

"My thoughts exactly." Mr. Hamilton nodded, looking at Mr. Gracie. "Your oldest son is becoming a very respectable young man, Archibald."

"What about me?" said Archie. "Am I respectable?"

"Archie!" exclaimed Mrs. Gracie, relieved to see

Mr. Hamilton laughing.

"If you learn from your older brother, you'll be respectable too when you're William's age," Mr. Hamilton said to Archie.

"Papa, can I help you raise the blue flag to let the captain of the *Virginia* know that Mr. Hamilton is here?" Archie asked.

"Of course, Archie," said Mr. Gracie. "But first I'd like to meet with Mr. Hamilton in my study."

WHILE HIS FATHER TALKED TO Mr. Hamilton at his desk, William removed one of the copies of cargo list he had prepared for Mr. Hamilton. As much as William admired Mr. Hamilton, he wished he had come earlier in the week. William was pre-occupied with his little brother and the mysterious stranger Archie said he met. The secret passageway still had to be explored. Could Archie have really seen someone? Or had he made the whole thing up?

"If we continue trading with England and France against Jefferson's wishes," Mr. Gracie was pondering, "will we be doing something illegal?"

Mr. Hamilton shook his head, looking thoughtful. "We have an interesting trade opportunity here," he said, "and we are entirely within the law. Jefferson will just have to accept it."

"That's good news," said Mr. Gracie. "Despite what President Jefferson says, I feel it's important to keep good relations with all of our trading partners."

William tried to pay attention to what the two men were talking about, but he found it difficult. It was hard enough to concentrate on his own work. Through the open window, he heard Eliza and Sarah picking vegetables in the garden with Mrs. Gracie.

"Are you finished yet, William?" Mr. Gracie asked, an hour later.

"I will be in a minute or so," William said, quickly finishing up the last few entries. Then he handed the list to Mr. Hamilton who thanked him.

"You have excellent penmanship, William," said Mr. Hamilton. William thanked him. "Now let's go meet with Captain Stewart. The three men left the small parlor study and met Archie in the front hall.

"Can I help raise the blue flag?" Archie asked again with excitement.

"Yes, Archie," Mr. Gracie said. And the four of them went outside. The blue flag was raised above the porch to let the captain of the *Virginia* know that Mr. Hamilton had arrived.

"Do you want to come down to the water with us, Archie?" Mr. Hamilton asked.

Archie shook his head. "I want to go inside and look for my ghost friend. I want to thank him for being so nice."

William glared at his younger brother, wishing he'd know when to be quiet. Up until now, his father seemed to have forgotten about Archie's confession at breakfast. As much as he wanted to ask Archie about Stefan, he didn't want to upset his father any more than he already had.

"Who is this ghost friend of yours?" Mr. Hamilton asked, his blue eyes twinkling.

"Enough of this ghost nonsense, Archibald Jr.," Mr. Gracie said sternly. "We'll talk about it after Mr. Hamilton has left." He started to walk down toward the river, waving at Captain Stewart who was already in a rowboat being rowed to shore.

"Actually, Archibald," Mr. Hamilton said, looking intrigued. "I'd really like to hear more about this ghost if you don't mind."

Looking surprised, Mr. Gracie shrugged. "Then come walk down with us, Archie."

"Can we come, Papa?" Eliza called from the garden.

"The more the merrier," said Mr. Gracie, gesturing for his wife to come too. "The captain will have quite a welcome."

As they all walked down toward the water, the rowboat was still several yards from shore. When they reached the dock by the bathing pavilion, Mr. Hamilton looked at Archie.

"Tell us more about your ghost friend, Archie," Mr. Hamilton said. William admired Mr. Hamilton for the soft spot he had for children.

"The ghost's name is Stefan," Archie explained. "When I fell through the secret passageway door, Stefan caught me. He was big like Papa. He was nice to me and lit a candle so I wouldn't be afraid. Then, when I saw Eliza's grammar book, I said I would bring it back to her."

"I was *sure* I had brought it here," Eliza said smugly.

Suddenly, Archie looked puzzled. "Do ghosts study grammar, Mr. Hamilton?"

"What makes you so sure this was a ghost, Archie?" Mr. Hamilton asked, smiling.

"I don't think he's a ghost, Mr. Hamilton," William said. "That was Sarah's idea." Mr. Hamilton looked at Sarah as Captain Stewart approached the group.

"I thought the ghost of Mrs. Walton, the woman who used to live at Horn's Hook, was haunting us so we'd leave," Sarah explained. "But from what Archie says, it seems as if the ghost's actually a man."

"I don't think it sounds like a ghost at all," Eliza said to Sarah. "I think we have a man living in our secret passageway."

By now, Mr. Gracie and Mr. Hamilton were so enraptured by Archie's story that they forgot to turn to greet Captain Stewart. William, however, nodded to the captain who didn't seem to mind at all. He, like the others, became interested as Archie continued his story.

"When I said I was going to bring Eliza her grammar book, Stefan, the ghost—I mean, the man—disappeared. Then I couldn't find the door to get back into the basement, so I started pounding on the wall," Archie said.

"By then we were already looking for Archie in other places," said William.

"How did you find the secret door in the first place?" asked Captain Stewart.

Surprised by the new voice, Mr. Gracie and Mr. Hamilton turned to the captain and apologized for not having greeted him properly.

"I'm just as interested in this story as you are,"

the captain said, smiling. "So how did you find the
secret door?

Archie explained how the four of them had
knocked on and felt around the wall.

"Papa told us the Waltons had built the passageway in case they had to escape," Sarah said.

"And I realized that the quickest escape from our house would be from the east wall of the basement to the river," William said.

"Good thinking, William," said Captain Stewart.

"Are you still angry with me, Papa?" Archie asked.

"I'm only angry that you children went into the basement when I told you not to," said Mr. Gracie, "but I must admit, I'm fascinated with . . . "

The captain interrupted Mr. Gracie. "Did Stefan talk funny?" he asked.

Archie thought for a moment. "Yes, I think so," he said. "But he didn't say very much."

"I don't feel comfortable having a strange man in our basement," Mrs. Gracie said. "I wonder if he's dangerous."

"I have a feeling he's not dangerous at all," said the captain. "It sounds to me as if he's a stowaway—maybe Hessian."

"Hessian?" asked Sarah, wondering what that meant.

"Yes," said Captain Stewart, "during the war many men from places like Hesse-Cassel and Hesse-Haupt in central Europe offered their services to fight for the King of England—for a fee, of course."

"Apparently many of them have settled here since the war," said Mr. Hamilton. "Let's go see for ourselves." And they all set off for the house.

11

AS THEY CLIMBED THE HILL TOWARD THE house, Captain Stewart did most of the talking. "We've been bothered by Hessian stowaways ever since the war ended. Many of the soldiers liked what they saw here in America. And, as Mr. Hamilton said, many of them either stayed or found ways of returning.

"But how would one of them have found the secret passageway into our house?" asked William.

"Many of the soldiers who were stationed here during the war probably heard stories of the underground passage," the captain explained. "If you don't mind, Mr. Gracie, I'll go down and see what I can find."

"Can I come too?" William asked. "I'd like to see what the passage looks like."

"I'd rather you didn't, William," said Mrs. Gracie. "Let's see what Captain Stewart finds."

"I don't think you have anything to worry about, Mrs. Gracie," said Mr. Hamilton, opening the front door for the others. "It sounds as if this man would be more afraid of us than we are of him."

"Exactly," said the captain, entering the house, "if my suspicions are right."

As soon as they were all inside, William lit a

lantern and led the others toward the basement door and down the rickety steps to the brick floor.

"Since it's not dangerous, I'd like to go into the secret passageway too," said Eliza.

"Me too," said Sarah, "though I hope it's not as scary as this basement."

"It is," said Archie. "But that doesn't bother me. I want to go. Stefan already knows me."

Mr. Hamilton laughed. "It sounds as though the two of you are on first-name basis."

"Children!" Mr. Gracie said. "It's already been decided. Captain Stewart and William will go."

"All right," said Archie, "but be nice to Stefan and try not to scare him away."

"Shh, let's try not to make any noise," William said as he led them to the wall right behind the wine cellar. They tried to walk as quietly as possible on the brick floor. This time William knew exactly where to find the secret door. He knelt down, pushed the wall, and the door opened easily. Carrying the lantern, he crawled into the tunnel with the captain close behind him. There, in front of him, was a plank of wood resting on two large stones. On this makeshift table were several of the missing items: his quill, Eliza's grammar book, a plate with a few crumbs, a small brown parcel with Archie's name on it, and a piece of parchment, which was no longer blank. William shined the lantern on the paper and saw that it was addressed to Archie.

"What does it say?" asked Captain Stewart, who looked very uncomfortable at having to crouch down.

"It's addressed to Archie," William said. "I don't think he'll be able to read this handwriting but I think he should be present when it's read. Let's leave these things here and go to the other end of the passageway."

"Good idea," said Captain Stewart, following William through the dim tunnel.

Once they had gone a few feet, the ceiling became

higher and they were both able to walk comfortably through to the other side. It took them less than five minutes to reach a solid wall at the other end. They could hear the sound of water on the other side.

"Push," said the captain.

William pushed and they both found themselves on the dock where they had been standing less than fifteen minutes earlier. William made sure to put a heavy stick in the doorway to prop it open. Captain Stewart waved to the sailor, who sat near the rowboat looking confused.

"No one's here," William said. "Let's go back to the others and find out what the letter says." He led the way back toward the basement end of the passageway. Captain Stewart helped him carry out the items that Stefan had borrowed.

"Where's Stefan?" Archie asked as William and the captain, once again, came through the secret doorway.

"I think he left," the captain said.

Archie looked disappointed.

"But he left this letter for you, Archie," William said, holding up the note. He decided to keep the parcel a secret until the letter was read.

"Let's read it up in the parlor," said Mrs. Gracie. "It's dark down here."

Excited to hear what the letter said, they all hurried up to the parlor where Lizzie was watching Robert and Hettie build a castle out of wooden blocks. She listened with the others, who sat on chairs, as William read the letter:

Dear Archie,

I want to thank you and your family for use of your house though you did not know I was here. It was wonderful to have place to stay during my first days back in America—especially since I was very seasick when I arrived. (I am not very good sailor.)

I am returning everything I borrowed except for food I took. To pay for that, I have left you a small gift from my village. Please let Eliza and William know that I am forever grateful for use of grammar book, quill, and paper. Without them, I wouldn't have known enough English to write letter! The blue and white blanket kept me warm at night and Lizzie's sweets were better than anything I have ever tasted. Please tell Sarah I am sorry for frightening her when I ran past her. I did not know you were coming until I saw you. I had to get back to passageway where I stayed.

I must admit I overhear some of your conversations. I wanted to join in. I also heard story of how much the Waltons loved this house. I learned about the secret underground passageway during the war. Living in a country that's not your own can be very lonely, but I knew that I wanted to return from Hesse-Cassel and come back to the United States of America.

I wish to find place away from the city where I can farm some land. I hope I can help another newcomer like you helped me.

Good-bye, Archie. It was nice to meet you even though our visit was very brief.

Your friend,
Stefan, the Ghost of Gracie Mansion

(I am sorry if I disappointed Sarah because I am not the ghost of Mrs. Walton, but I am sure Mrs. Walton would be happy to know the Gracie family is here. You are very nice family.)

"What a nice letter!" Mrs. Gracie said, looking relaxed for the first time in weeks.

"I'm glad it was him and not Mrs. Walton's ghost," Sarah said. "It makes a better story." The others laughed.

"What's wrong, Archie?" Mr. Gracie asked, noticing his son's confused expression.

"Where's the small gift he left me?" Archie asked, looking at the items on the table which were all familiar.

"Here it is, Archie," William said, smiling. He handed the small brown parcel to his younger brother.

Archie grabbed the parcel, unwrapped it, and pulled out a small, porcelain clock. "It's just a clock," Archie said.

"It's a very special clock, Archie," Mr. Hamilton said. "It's from Europe. You'll appreciate it when you're older."

Archie shrugged and handed the clock to Mrs. Gracie. "Can I go play in the secret passageway?" he asked.

Mrs. Gracie looked at Mr. Gracie and Mr. Gracie

looked at William and Captain Stewart. "Is it safe enough for the children to play in?" he asked.

William and the captain nodded. "Just as long as the children are careful not to fall into the river at the opposite end."

"Did you go all the way to the river?" Eliza asked. Everyone had been so interested in what the letter had said that they'd forgotten to ask about the secret passageway.

"All the way there and back," William said. "It's not very long at all."

WILLIAM, CAPTAIN STEWART, AND the other Gracies said good-bye to Mr. Hamilton, who said it was the most exciting day he had had in a while.

"I'm sorry I didn't get a chance to go over the legal procedures with you, Captain Stewart," Mr. Hamilton said as he shook the captain's hand. "But once Archie started talking about ghosts, I just had to learn more. I've always been a curious man."

"That's quite all right," said the captain, good-naturedly. "I, too, am fascinated with the way things turned out."

"Don't worry about a thing, Alexander," Mr. Gracie said. "I'll bring Captain Stewart up to date on all legal matters."

"Very well," said Mr. Hamilton. Once he had climbed into the carriage, he turned to William. "Thank you for all your hard work, young man. I suggest that you relax for the rest of the day. Have fun with Archie and your sisters. You're only young once."

For the first time, William didn't feel insulted at being called young. Instead, he felt happy about having no responsibilities for the rest of the day. He even looked forward to spending time with Archie, Eliza, and Sarah.

As soon as the carriage was gone, Mrs. Gracie invited the captain into the house for tea while William, Eliza, Sarah, and Archie hurried back to the basement. Despite the dankness and the cobwebs, they spent the rest of the day going in and out of the secret—or not–so–secret—passageway wondering what it had been like for a grown man to have spent so much time there.

"Captain Stewart is leaving!" Sarah called from the doorway near the water.

William followed Archie and Eliza toward Sarah, and they all stepped out onto the dock where Mr. and Mrs. Gracie stood talking.

As they all stood on the dock waving to the captain and the sailors as they rowed back to the *Virginia*, William realized that he was in no rush to get back to the city. He liked being at Gracie Mansion. He liked working there with his father and playing with his brother and sisters. But when he did go back, he'd have quite a story to tell Jasper and the other messengers.

There really was a Gracie Family just like the one in the story. They did live in the house that is now known as Gracie Mansion and is now the official home of New York City Mayors and their families.

Archibald Gracie was a generous man who contributed greatly to the life of the city. He was an important part of the early business life of the city helping to found The Bank of New York and the New York Stock Exchange. He helped develop the first public schools and the first public hospital. He was also instrumental in the establishment of the New-York Historical Society. He was never directly involved with politics like his lawyer Alexander Hamilton but he supported the Federalist point of view and provided some of the money for the newspaper that supported their cause.

It is also true that the policies that President Jefferson carried out were seriously damaging to Archibald Gracie and other shipping merchants like him. Jefferson and the Congress passed the Embargo Act making it illegal to ship to England and France. This put Mr. Gracie at a terrible disadvantage and eventually he lost most of the fortune he had made. But his generous legacy is still part of New York City in all its important institutions. While the house may continue to change as it did in the Gracie Family time, it will always be called Gracie Mansion and the Mayors of New York City will continue to live there.